WHeN We GO CAMPING

SALLY SUTTON   Illustrated by CAT CHAPMAN

WALKER BOOKS

AND SUBSIDIARIES

LONDON • BOSTON • SYDNEY • AUCKLAND

When we go camping, we bang in the pegs,
Bang in the pegs, bang in the pegs.
Guy ropes are tricky; they trip up our legs!

Smacketty
tappetty bopp-io.

When we go camping, we zip down the door,
Zip down the door, zip down the door.
We tie up the windows and lie on the floor.

Zippetty
zappetty flopp-io.

When we go camping, we make lots of friends,
Make lots of friends, make lots of friends.
We race them and chase them until the day ends.

Jumpetty
bumpetty gigg-lio.

When we go camping, we fish for our dinner,
Fish for our dinner, fish for our dinner.
We throw back the ones that are smaller and thinner.

Flippetty
         flappetty jigg-lio.

When we go camping, we shoo away flies,

Shoo away flies, shoo away flies.

They buzz round our heads and our knees and our thighs.

Slappetty whacketty swash-io.

When we go camping, we carry the water,

Carry the water, carry the water.

We clean all the dishes, 'cause Mum says we oughta.

Scrubbetty

rubbetty wash-io.

When we go camping, we bathe in the sea,
Bathe in the sea, bathe in the sea.
We're salty and sandy and shiny and free.

Splishetty
splashetty dripp-io.

When we go camping, we boil up the billy,
Boil up the billy, boil up the billy.
A lovely warm drink is so good when you're chilly!

slurpetty
          sloppetty sipp-io.

When we go camping, we pee in a long-drop,
Pee in a long-drop, pee in a long-drop.
Eek! It stinks! Let's make it a quick stop.

Tinkletty
sprinkletty shriek-io.

When we go camping, we sing round the fire,
Sing round the fire, sing round the fire.
Grandpa sings lower and Grandma sings higher.

Hummetty strummetty squeak-io.

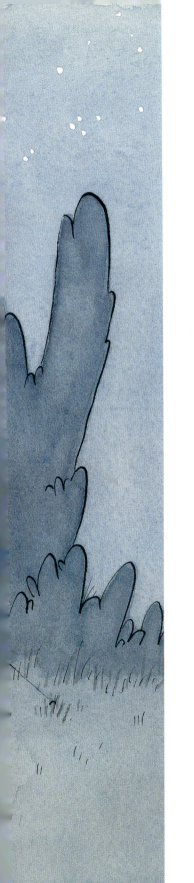

When we go camping, we hear something funny,
Hear something funny, hear something funny.
Tigers? Or monsters? Or maybe ... a bunny!

Snuffletty
wuffletty roar-io.

When we go camping, we sleep through the night,
Sleep through the night, sleep through the night.
And dream of adventures we'll have when it's light.

Hushetty

shushetty snore-io.